# Mitchell
## on the MOON

### R. W. Alley

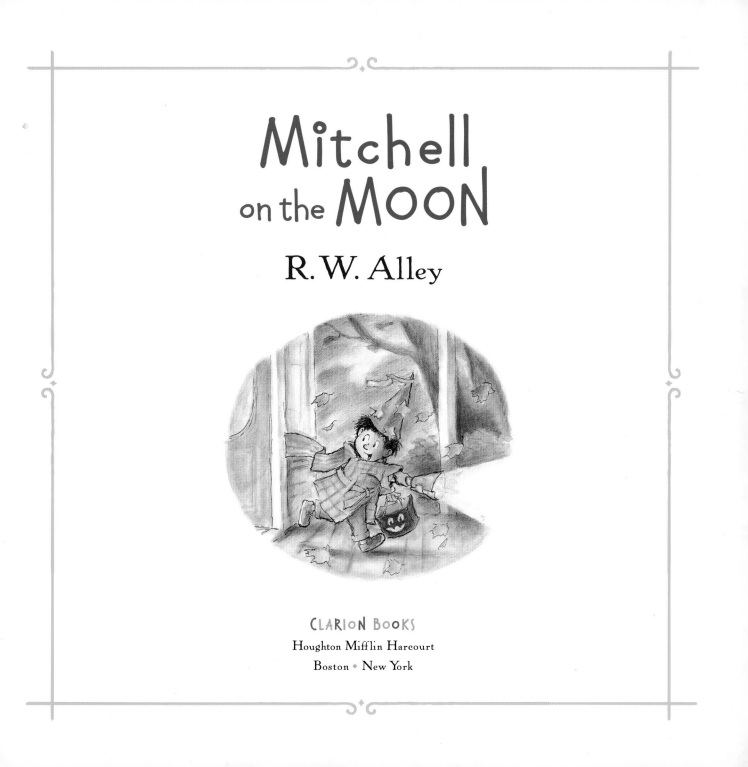

CLARION BOOKS

Houghton Mifflin Harcourt

Boston ◆ New York

Clarion Books
3 Park Avenue
New York, New York 10016

Clarion Books is an imprint of Houghton Mifflin Harcourt Publishing Company.

www.hmhco.com

The illustrations in this book were done in ink, pencils, watercolors,
gouaches, and acrylics on Bristol board paper.
The text was set in Julius Primary.

Library of Congress Cataloging-in-Publication is available.
ISBN: 978-0-547-90703-1

Manufactured in China
SCP 10 9 8 7 6 5 4 3 2 1
4500600057

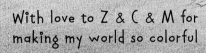

With love to Z & C & M for
making my world so colorful

**ONE** windy fall evening,
Mitchell was leading the way.
Until . . . Gretchen said, "STOP!
The moon is disappearing."
"Uh-oh," said Mitchell.

"Now it's too dark and spooky to go out," said Gretchen.
"It's just clouds," said Clark.
"The moon is still there," said Annabelle.

But Mitchell said, "Gretchen is right.
The moon is in trouble.
Only I, the Sorcerer of Space, can
save the moon."

"The roly-polys and I will help," said Gretchen.
"We'll be your sidekicks!"
"No," said Mitchell. "Too dangerous.

Only the Sorcerer of Space can ride
the Moon Ladder of Magic and Mystery."

"ZOOMITY UP!" commanded Mitchell.
The moon ladder blasted off
into outer space.

**"ZAPPITY SNAP!"**

Mitchell blew aside molten meteors
with his lightning wand.

The moon ladder zoomed faster and faster.
"Uh-oh," said Mitchell. "Too fast! It's out of control.
ZIPPITY SNATCH!"
The lightning wand's beam lassoed the moon
just in time.

"Time for the Sorcerer of Space
to save the moon!" said Mitchell.
He slid to where the moon was vanishing.

"GADZOOKS! Jack O' Jerks are biting away bits of the moon like candy. It will be gone in no time." Suddenly . . .

"Let's get 'em!" Gretchen shouted.

"Hey!" said Mitchell. "I didn't know I had a sidekick."

Gretchen slipped and slid down the slippery moon.

"Help!"

"Yummy," said the Jack O' Jerks.

"Really?" said Mitchell.
"Now my sidekick needs saving?"
"Yes, please," squeaked Gretchen.
"Tasty," said the Jack O' Jerks.

"SNIZZLE SCOOT!
BLAMMITY BOOT!"
Mitchell's lightning wand
whirled the Jack O' Jerks round
and round, until they went . . .

And Mitchell and Gretchen tumbled topsy-turvy.

Gravity pulled the munched moon
back together. The moon was saved.
"YIKES!" said Gretchen. "We're lost in space."

"The Sorcerer of Space is never lost," said Mitchell.

They rode the lightning-wand beam all the way home.

"Hooray! The moon is saved!" said Gretchen.
"No thanks to you two," said Mitchell to Clark
and Annabelle.
"Good thing you had a sidekick!" said Gretchen.
"Hmm," said Mitchell.

Then, after a snack of roasted pumpkin seeds,
they headed out into the moon-bright evening.